Tales from
Christmas
Wood

For Zoe and Daniel   S.S
To Mum, Dad, Jessica, and Joseph   J.N.G.

Text copyright © 2015 Suzy Senior
Illustrations copyright © 2015 James Newman Gray
This edition copyright © 2015 Lion Hudson

Published by Lion Children's Books
an imprint of
Lion Hudson plc
Wilkinson House, Jordan Hill Road,
Oxford OX2 8DR, England
www.lionhudson.com/lionchildrens

ISBN 978 0 7459 6546 8

First edition 2015

A catalogue record for this book is available from the British Library

Printed and bound in Malaysia, June 2015, LH18

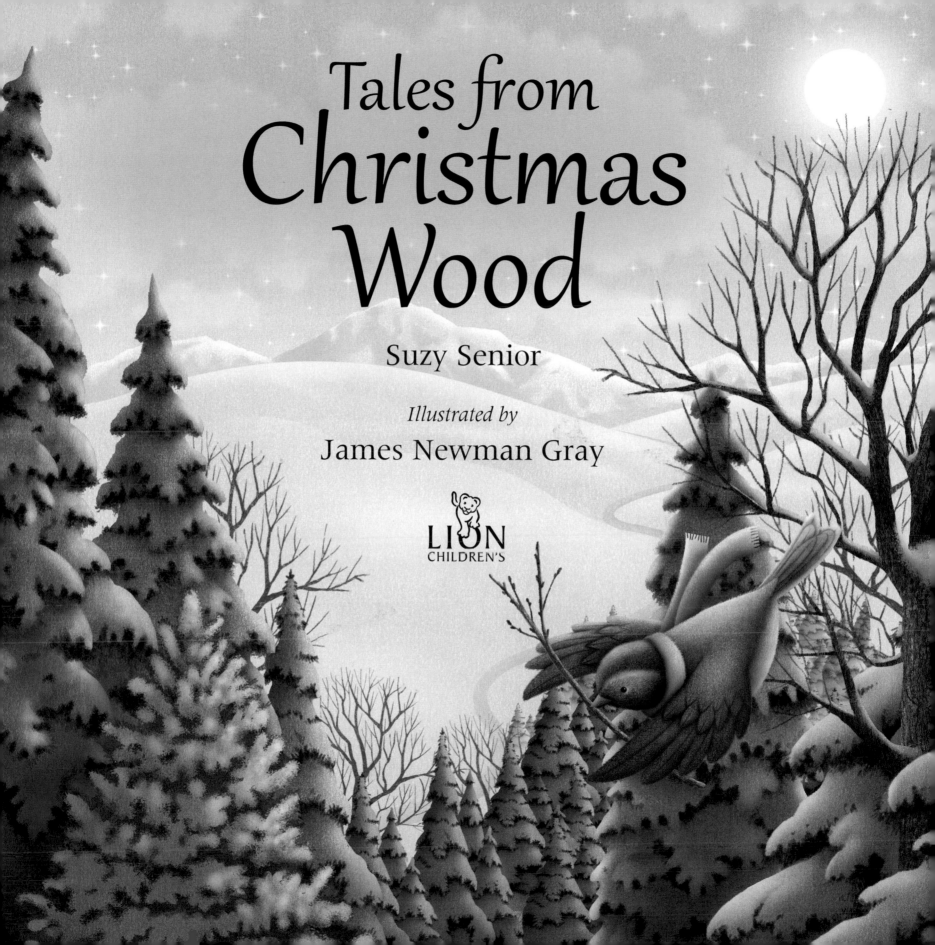

Tales from
Christmas
Wood

Suzy Senior

Illustrated by

James Newman Gray

LION
CHILDREN'S

Badger Finds a Friend

Badger wasn't looking for Christmas Wood. She was just passing by. She turned a corner, crossed a bumpy bridge – and there it was!
Badger was wonderstruck. "I'm going to live here!" she decided.
She started work on a tunnel and quickly settled in. Everything was perfect… until Badger tried to make some friends.

First, Rosie Rabbit hopped by with her brothers.
"Good morning," yawned Badger.
The rabbits froze. "Look at those TEETH!" squealed
Rosie, and the rabbits shot into the bushes.

Later, some wood mice were having a picnic.
"Lovely day," called Badger.
Tiny Mouse grabbed his Mama's paw and a slice of Grandma's cake. "A stripy
monster!" he cried, and the mice dived under a log.
The next day was just the same. EVERYONE seemed to be frightened of Badger.

Finally, Badger had an idea. "I'll find a Wise-Old-Owl," she thought. "I'm sure they could help me find a friend."

"Hello," she called to an owl, "are you the Wise-Old-Owl?"

"Ah… sorry, no," replied the owl. "He moved away ages ago. I'm just 'Owl'. Are you new around here?" he asked cheerfully.

Badger told Owl everything. She really wanted to make some friends, but it was difficult being new and bigger than everyone else.

Owl nodded kindly. It could be hard to make friends when everyone thought you were the Wise-Old-Owl, too.

Then Owl's friend Fidgety Fox popped by, and they all played hide-and-seek.
They had a fantastic time, until Badger had to go home for tea!

"Come back tomorrow," called Owl. "By the way, I'm sorry I couldn't help you
with your problem."

Badger waved at her new friends.

"Oh, I think you have," she laughed. "Thank you! See you tomorrow."

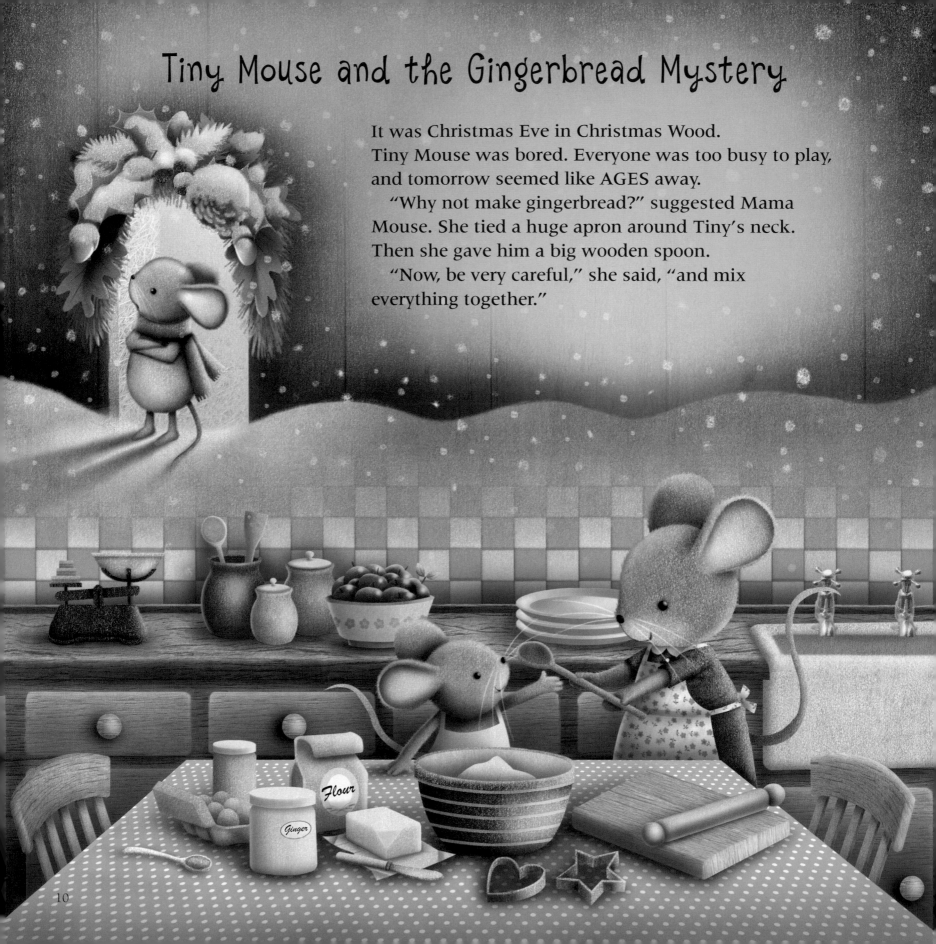

Tiny Mouse and the Gingerbread Mystery

It was Christmas Eve in Christmas Wood.
Tiny Mouse was bored. Everyone was too busy to play,
and tomorrow seemed like AGES away.

"Why not make gingerbread?" suggested Mama
Mouse. She tied a huge apron around Tiny's neck.
Then she gave him a big wooden spoon.

"Now, be very careful," she said, "and mix
everything together."

Tiny Mouse stirred carefully until his little paws were tired. Then (just to check it was nice) he ate a blob of the mixture. It WAS nice... but maybe it needed a pinch more sugar? That was better. He tasted a little more. It WAS nice... but maybe a pinch more ginger? Even better. He tasted a little more... then a little more. Yes! Now it was just right. His friends were going to love this gingerbread.

Very carefully, Tiny scooped out some dough and squashed it flat. He cut it into a star-shaped cookie.

Tiny grinned. That looked great.

But when he scooped again, nothing came out! He peered carefully into the bowl.

"Oh!" he gasped.

The bowl was completely empty.

"Mama!" he squeaked. "Where has all the mixture gone?"

Mama Mouse looked into the bowl and frowned. She looked at Tiny's worried little face. Then she looked at his sticky little whiskers.

"I think it might be in your tummy," she said quietly.

"Oh no!" cried Tiny Mouse. "How did that happen?"

"Never mind," smiled Mama Mouse. "I'll get tidied up while you go over to see Grandma."

At Grandma's house, Tiny snuggled onto her lap. He told her about the disappearing gingerbread. "It really was an accident," he said sadly, "and I'm so sorry, because now there aren't any Christmas cookies to give to our friends."

Then he had a thought. "Grandma, please could I try again?" he asked.

"What a lovely idea," she said.

She tied a huge apron around Tiny's neck. Then she gave him a big wooden spoon.

"Now, be very careful…" she said, "… and try not to eat it this time."

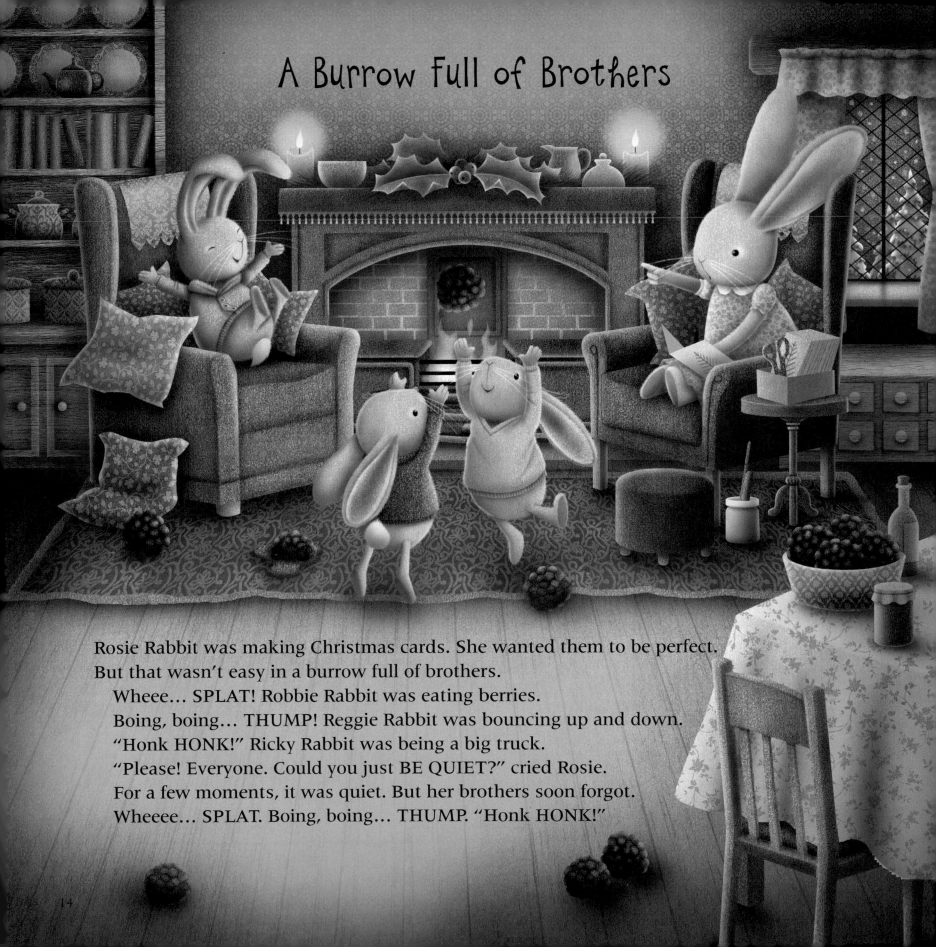

A Burrow Full of Brothers

Rosie Rabbit was making Christmas cards. She wanted them to be perfect.
But that wasn't easy in a burrow full of brothers.

Wheee… SPLAT! Robbie Rabbit was eating berries.

Boing, boing… THUMP! Reggie Rabbit was bouncing up and down.

"Honk HONK!" Ricky Rabbit was being a big truck.

"Please! Everyone. Could you just BE QUIET?" cried Rosie.

For a few moments, it was quiet. But her brothers soon forgot.

Wheeee… SPLAT. Boing, boing… THUMP. "Honk HONK!"

Rosie felt angry. "No one listens to me," she thought. "Nobody even cares about me." She threw down her paintbrush and stomped out.

It was cold in Christmas Wood. Rosie's breath made clouds in the air. She felt like a brave explorer. Soon, fat snowflakes started to fall. Rosie twirled, catching them on her whiskers.

But then the snow changed. It fell faster and faster. It blew into her ears and up her nose.

"Oh help!" thought Rosie.

"Rosie, do you want a berry?" called Robbie.
"I haven't licked it."

But there was no answer.

"Rosie, I bumped my head,"
whimpered Reggie.

But there was no answer.

"Rosie, can I help you paint?" asked Ricky.
Still no answer.

"Rosie's not here!" gasped Robbie. He peeped outside
and saw... SNOW.

Suddenly it was very quiet. No splat, no boing, no honk.
Just three worried bunnies.

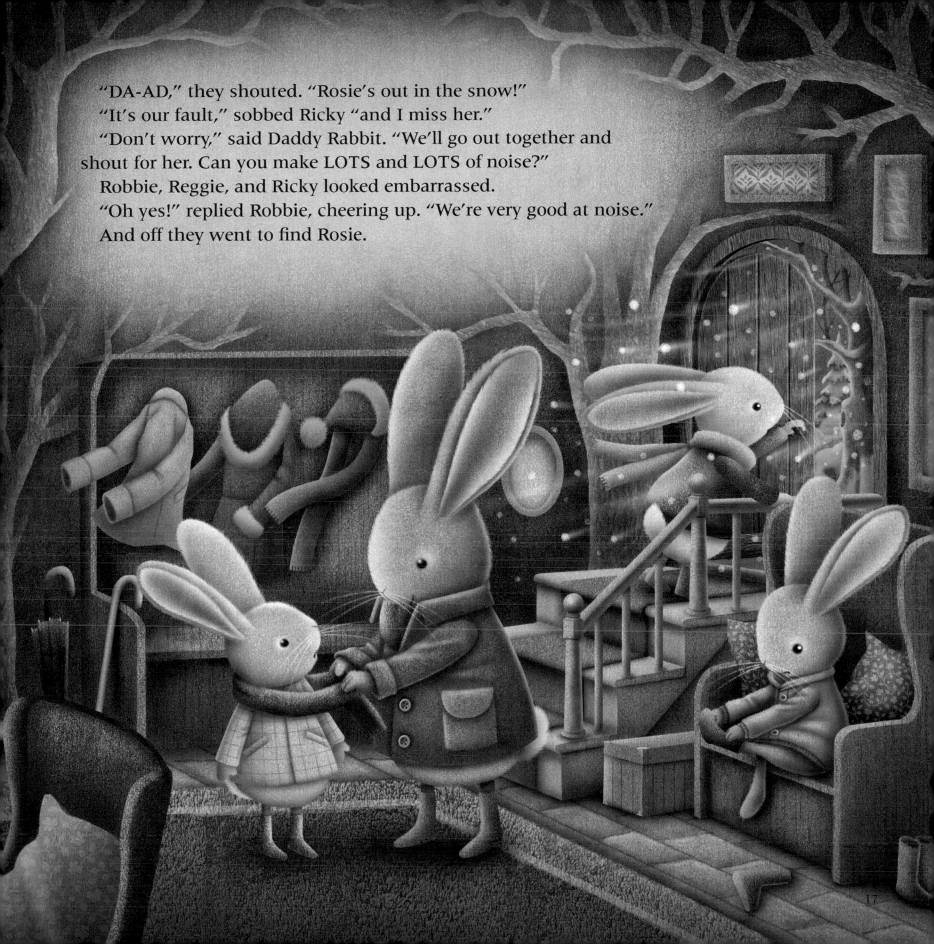

"DA-AD," they shouted. "Rosie's out in the snow!"

"It's our fault," sobbed Ricky "and I miss her."

"Don't worry," said Daddy Rabbit. "We'll go out together and shout for her. Can you make LOTS and LOTS of noise?"

Robbie, Reggie, and Ricky looked embarrassed.

"Oh yes!" replied Robbie, cheering up. "We're very good at noise."

And off they went to find Rosie.

The Amazing Robin

Robin zoomed across Christmas Wood. He swooped under the frosty branches.

"Don't worry! The Amazing Robin will save you!" he cried.

He caught a falling twig and landed gently on the ground.

"There you are. All safe," he said grandly. The twig said nothing. (It was just a twig.)

Robin loved playing "heroes".

"One day," he thought, "when I'm older, I'll be a REAL hero. I'll be fearless like Fidgety Fox. I'll be big like Badger, and as wise as Owl!"

Then he sighed. He could fly, but he was just a little bird. How could HE help anyone?

Suddenly it began to snow. The flakes fell faster and faster.

Robin snuggled into his feathers. He tucked himself further into his holly tree.

Then he heard a sneeze: "Aaachoo!" It looked like Rosie Rabbit, disappearing through the bushes. She didn't come back.

"She's all by herself!" thought Robin. "On Christmas Eve, too. Perhaps she's lost."

Robin dashed through the whirling snow to Badger's house. Robin was a bit scared of Badger, but he really needed help. So Robin thought about Rosie lost in the snow and suddenly felt much braver.

Badger and her friend Owl came straight away. They followed Robin through the snow until BUMP! – they almost fell over the Rabbit family.

"We're looking for Rosie," cried Daddy Rabbit. "She's out in the snow!"

"Don't worry," called Badger. "Just follow Robin! He thought he saw Rosie, so he came to fetch help."

"Thank you, Robin," cried Daddy Rabbit. "That was very kind." He looked nervously at Badger's teeth. "And very brave too! You're quite a hero."

Robin blushed proudly. His face turned as red as his chest. For once, he hadn't even thought about being a hero.

Perhaps he didn't need to be more like anybody else. Perhaps he could do amazing things already.

Just maybe – he realized – he had all the superpowers he needed… just as he was.

A Christmas Eve Adventure

Fidgety Fox was looking for adventure: a special Christmas Eve sort of adventure. He was wearing his best adventuring scarf, and singing his best adventuring song. Now he just needed something exciting to happen.

He checked under the holly bushes. No adventure there – just prickles.

He looked inside the hollow tree. No adventure there – just beetles.

He peeked into the barn. No adventure there – just...

... a huge brown MONSTER with massive KNOBBLY KNEES!
He backed away quickly. That was the wrong kind of exciting.

23

Fidgety raced around the corner and – OOOFF – straight into Badger. Badger bumped into Owl. Owl tripped over the Rabbit family. Robin dived out of the way. And they all landed in a heap in the snow.

"Quickly, get up," panted Fidgety. "There's a MONSTER in the barn!"

"A monster?" wondered Robin. He didn't think there were any such things as monsters.

He peered through a gap in the door. There WAS a strange creature in the barn. It was tall and brown and had knobbly knees. But it didn't look very fierce. Robin gave a gentle cough. It didn't seem to notice.

But something else DID…

Something rustled in the hay, just inside. Out popped one pointy ear; then another pointy ear…

And then the rest of ROSIE RABBIT!

"We've found Rosie!" cried Robin. The Monster was forgotten as Robbie, Reggie, and Ricky Rabbit tumbled into the doorway. They threw themselves onto Rosie and hugged her so much that they almost squashed her.

"I'm sorry we were noisy."

"Please come back!"

"We missed you, Rosie."

"I'm sorry I went off in a huff," said Rosie. "And I'm so glad you found me. I missed you too." She kissed them all on their little noses.

Fidgety straightened his best adventuring scarf and chuckled at the jumble of rabbits. He had found a special Christmas Eve sort of adventure after all.

A Very Busy Barn

Tiny Mouse poked his head out of the mousehole in the barn wall. His whiskers twitched with excitement. His gingerbread cookies were finally ready, and he couldn't wait to give them out.

Just outside he saw EVERYONE: Daddy Rabbit and the little Rabbits, Fidgety Fox, Badger, Robin, and Owl.

"Happy Christmas Eve!" cried Tiny. "Come in and get warm!"

Everyone looked at the mousehole. It looked a bit of a squeeze.

"No – in here!" laughed Tiny. He led them right inside the barn. And what did they see…?

A big glowing star hung from the rafters. Underneath were some sheep and a donkey… and a tall, brown camel *with knobbly knees*.

But strangest of all, there was a baby boy and his family. He was all tucked up in the manger. Three men in fancy clothes carried beautiful gifts for the baby. "Don't worry," said Tiny. "They're all made of wood." He gave the donkey a poke to prove it.

"THAT's a Nativity scene," he said importantly. "It's all about what happened on the very first Christmas night. People come here and remember why they're celebrating. Everybody loves to see the special baby. They all sing songs and sometimes they bring gifts for each other too!"

Tiny couldn't wait ANY longer…

"… and I've got a GIFT for all of YOU!" he squeaked happily.

He shyly handed everyone gingerbread cookies.

Badger's was shaped just like the glowing star above the Nativity scene.

"These cookies are wonderful," she said. "Thank you, Tiny Mouse!"

Everybody agreed, and Tiny felt so happy he thought he might burst.

Robin started to sing a Christmassy tune, and their cheery voices soon
filled the barn.

Badger smiled around warmly at all her friends.
She already loved living in Christmas Wood.
But celebrating CHRISTMAS in Christmas Wood was the best bit yet.

Other titles from Lion Children's Books

Babushka   *Dawn Casey & Amanda Hall*

Little Bear's Sparkly Christmas   *Julia Stone & Angela Muss*

The Christmas Story for Little Angels   *Julia Stone & Dubravka Kolanovic*

The Little Christmas Tree   *Andrea Skevington & Lorna Hussey*